Feminized & FULL-Filled

- An LGBTQ+, First Time, Feminization, Short-Read Romance

by Barbara Deloto and Thomas Newgen

To purchase another copy of this book, or to see our other books go to
https://www.amazon.com/Barbara-Deloto/e/B00J21HWA4/

A few of our other books
*Realizing Jessica - A Femboy Gets Fem and Discovers Inner Passions
and Love*
Desires- Fantasy Becomes Reality for an Occasional Crossdresser
Trannies - Two Guys Get Fem
Jessica's Turn: A Gender-Bending LGBT Romance
Frat House - A Gender-Bending LGBT Romance
*Finishing School - A Boy Is Sent to a Girls' Finishing School - An LGBT
Romance*
All Dolled Up: A Student Gets Fem - An LGBT Romance
Sissy Boyfriend
Being Candy
Paying My Dues
Virtual Vacation
Filling in For Her
His New Dress
Her Gift to Him
Telling Her
Feminized to Win
Crossdreaming
Feminized by Her
Taking it for the Team
Feminized Men: A Guide for Increased Joy in Crossdressing
Feminized Vacation
The House of Enchanted Feminization
Heirs to Heiresses
Connected
Our Gift to Each Other
Girlfriend
Insatiable
A New Taste for Life
Spellbound
Femboy Guild

1

I stared at the check. It was a lot of money. My mom had signed it in her beautiful feminine penmanship. I left the east coast conservative college my dad made me attend for three years and won a scholarship to a liberal, California college. Now my mom was helping me further the pursuit of my dreams. My eyes teared up.

I wiped them and read her letter again. "My dear sweet Lee, your father was upset by you leaving the college he picked for you, but *I* know it's for the best. He thought you'd be the ideal son and always wished that for you, but I always knew you weren't *son* material, but you still are ideal. I love you and wish you the best. Come visit me when you're comfortable to do so. Love, mom. X O." Her heartfelt love and hopes for me filled me with warmth.

The excuse I used to leave the old school was to pursue nuclear engineering, which the school I was at didn't have and the new school did. I was twenty-one and didn't have to listen to my dad anymore, it was the last year of my engineering education, and nuke fascinated me anyway. It fit my world view of connectedness and how things in the world were driven at the atomic and quantum levels.

Not that nuclear engineering could explain why I could sense how other people felt, or how things work out and are synchronistic and so on, but nuclear engineering was the closest *any* engineering could come to it. Who knew if I'd ever really go into the field, but any engineering degree was worth plenty on graduation and it was a great excuse to leave that oppressive college I was at and be me.

Dad wanted me to be tough, smart, and handsome, and marry a gorgeous wife and have lots of kids. Oh well, I was smart, but I'd never become the man he wanted.

Staring at the check, I thought about my next steps. Deposit it, of course. Send mom a thank you note so I don't cry on the phone with her and then... become who I wanted to become.

I walked into the kitchen of my rented house, paid for with scholarship funds, and poured myself an iced tea. I took an emergency smoke, a lighter, and a pad and pen from the kitchen junk drawer and walked out on the back porch of the old Victorian.

The scent of fresh cut grass and honeysuckle filled the air as I sat on the porch swing and lit my smoke. I sipped the tea. What to do. I'd have to go into the bank to deposit such a large amount. Then what? I crossed my smoothly shaved legs in my guy's jeans, bounced a foot, and set the swing in motion. I sniffed the dab of perfume on my wrist, took a drag on the smoke and blew it out, relishing the rush of the nicotine.

I gazed down at my black, tough guy tee-shirt and knew the clothes I was wearing now, I'd never wear again. This was it. I'd be who I wanted to be and today will be the first day of me being me. I penned a quick letter to mom and folded it up after drying my tears of gratitude for her.

I finished that smoke and even had another as an overwhelming sense of freedom infused me with every item I added to the list of what to get done today. Carpe diem!

2

It was only 4 o'clock, and I had accomplished my list. The new things that needed washing were in the dryer and the other things organized and put away. When the dryer was done, I'd become the new me.

I ran my hand through my new hairstyle. It was thick and luxurious and had waves and highlights. It was such a huge contrast to my usual mundane ponytail. I couldn't wait to be the girl I was inside.

I could kick myself for waiting so long. I masqueraded as a guy all these years and only *played* dress up when I could—like when my sister used to help me do when I was a teen, even after my dad caught us.

I was thrilled, anticipating my future, sipping my tea and bouncing a foot as I throbbed in my tightie-whities. I was doing it. My heart raced as I thought about going out in public. Not that I wouldn't pass. I pass better as a girl than a guy anyway, even without the proper clothes and accoutrements. My voice even leaned more toward a girl than a guy. I wasn't afraid of *that*, so why so nervous?

I wasn't sure. Maybe it was the novelty of it. Perhaps the fear of discovery, unlikely as it was. Maybe it was not ending up the perfect girl I wanted to be. I had all summer before I had to start school again and I had an excess of money, even after my shopping spree. I had to relax and just let myself become who I was.

I sniffed the honeysuckle and sipped my tea while considering my outfit choices and where to go. Who would I meet? Would it be a woman that I'd fall in love with, or would it only be men that would want to engage with me? What if a man did? What would I do? Who knew? I had no reservations about relationships with women or men, though I never had luck with girls. I told myself to just let the connectedness of the universe bring me my deepest desires. Feel it. Let it happen.

Taking a deep breath, I finished my tea and took the things out of the dryer, then put them away. I selected the outfit for the evening and placed it on the bed, complete with the shoes, purse, and jewelry.

The shower was exceptionally sensual as I ran the razor over the little stubble on my body, making my skin smooth and silky. I washed and conditioned my hair, removing the roughness from the hair coloring and perming.

Wrapping my hair in a towel, I painted my toenails and glued on matching, long, fake fingernails.

I dried and fluffed my hair, used my new makeup, eyeliner, mascara, eyeshadow, blush, and twenty-four-hour lipstick to make my face pop. My lips were luscious, my cheeks perky, and my eyes alive and bright. I couldn't stop the smile from filling my face as I let out a little squeal of delight.

I skipped into the room and sat on the bed. The sheer, suntan pantyhose I had cut a piece of the gusset out of slid up my legs, sending a shiver of delight through me. Next, the pale blue, silky panties with lace edging trapped my already hard shaft and shaved globes against my tummy. A matching bra with substantial gel breast forms gave me cleavage to die for. The simple flared denim miniskirt snapped around my waist and I snapped the front snaps down to the top of my thigh, leaving the others below open to reveal more leg.

A pale-blue lace-cap-sleeve, V-neck top formed to my breasts, and I adjusted it to cover the bra, except for the delicate lace edging. I slid into the one-inch-platform, six-inch-heeled, strappy, denim wedge heels and strapped them about my ankle. Fastening a blue beaded ankle bracelet about my ankle, I stood up and walked to the full-length mirror. I was now a towering five-foot-nine in my shoes and as I moved to and fro before the mirror, posing, moving, I swelled in my panties at the sight of the gorgeous girl before me.

Did that mean I was a guy and really wanted a girl for a partner? I did not know at that point and didn't think about it anymore. Daintily, I stepped over to the dresser and placed the three dangling earrings in each ear, loving the way they tinkled when I moved my head. I put on my necklace, bracelets, and rings, then sprayed perfume over my hair, on my legs, under my skirt and on my wrists and neck. The scent immersed me in femininity and completed my transformation into who I was.

Standing there proudly, I loaded my purse with my phone in its new blingy case, my license and credits cards in their new little pink wallet, and lipstick, perfume, mints, tissues, and pepper spray. Slinging it on my shoulder, I slung my short denim jacket on it, then I hooked a long nailed thumb over it. I stood straight and proud before the full-length mirror for one last inspection.

I had become the girl I always wanted to be. Now it was time to see exactly who that was. I throbbed uncontrollably in my panties and unconsciously massaged my hardness through my skirt as I gazed into my eyes. My eyes flitted around my face and hair... my breasts and legs. I licked my luscious lips and puckered them, then ran my tongue around them. I opened them and sucked my finger seductively.

My breath became choppy while my body tingled all over. I stopped sucking my thumb and caressed my heaving breasts, enjoying the reassuring weight of them on my chest. A whimper leaked from me. I stopped massaging myself, my knees weak. I leaned against the wall, facing the mirror, looking deeply into my eyes, seeing my soul's sensuality.

My voice automatically came out in its most feminine form, almost honey like as I heard, "Okay, Lee. Take a deep breath and relax now. It's time to go out in public and see who you are, *girl*." I laughed, my eyes bright with excitement.

I stepped back from the mirror for one last inspection. Although I throbbed uncontrollably beneath my skirt, it wasn't the least bit visible because of the flare of the skirt, even as my legs moved forward or back. That was a good thing because I knew I'd be this way all night long tonight.... unless.... well... I slipped out of control, or some nice person *took* me over the edge.

3

I held the railing, stepping off the porch gingerly and walked in minced steps in my high-heeled wedges down the walk to the sidewalk. I walked purposefully, my breasts tugging on my chest with each step, the breeze delightful on my legs and up my skirt, my hair flitting about my face and neck.

My perfume wafted to my nose, and my only maleness, which was very *girly* and *pretty* now, throbbed incessantly in my panties, in time with my steps. I laughed as I thought of it as my little girlfriend now as opposed to my manhood or little man. I breathed deep and held my head high as I passed the Victorians and made my way around the corner to the commercial area with bars and restaurants.

I checked them out for the first time, gazing inside and trying to find the right atmosphere. Something not too slimy, not too fancy, not for pickups, not just sports... and with some decent food. I was hungry for flavors as intense and sensual as I was right then.

A menu was in a window, and I stopped. The place was bright and airy, with skylights above the large square bar reaching to the back, and down-lights above the bar. Glittering glassware hung from the dark-stained wood and brass racks above the bar. The seats were padded on the backs and seats, and swiveled above the brass rails.

It was a comfortable and welcoming looking place with a decent looking young clientele all chatting and smiling. There were only two televisions above the bar and it obviously wasn't a sports bar, thank god. The bistro menu had raw oysters at a buck a shuck and a variety of small plates, tapas, and interesting drinks.

A hand landed on my shoulder and a lovely woman's voice said, "You'll love it. We're regulars here. No trouble at this place and the food is fantastic. Are you new to the area?"

I turned and her hand fell to her side. She stood next to a slight, good looking, and almost pretty, guy with long eyelashes and a smiling face. He seemed to be like I used to be before tonight, except with a magnificent smile. I hardly ever smiled before. I automatically smiled in response.

She was beaming in a white denim skirt, white V-neck tank top revealing plentiful cleavage, and wore white wedge heels with sheer glossy suntan pantyhose. The white contrasted with her darker skin and honey-red colored hair. She was exotic looking and very sexy, and I could sense both of their warm and friendly natures.

"Hi!" I happily said as I flipped my hair with my hand and tried to look my most welcoming. I put my hand out to her. "My name's Lee. I *am* new to the area. So this is *thee* place, huh?"

She nodded and shook my hand. "I'm Bree and this is my friend, Dree."

I turned to him and put my hand out. "Dree?"

He nodded and took my hand in his soft hand and gently shook mine. "Yup. I know it's odd. Dree. It means strong and manly." He laughed. "But it's really a girl's name, like Bree. Go figure. I guess my parents had a sense of humor, as did Mariel Hemingway, who named her daughter that."

"Nice to meet you, Dree... and Bree?"

"Right. Nice to meet you too, Lee. Please, come in with us and join us. I'm dying for a sensual drink and some sensual food."

"How weird. Me too. I was just thinking that while I was trying to decide where to go."

She laughed and tossed her hair. "I knew we had a lot in common." She put her arm around my shoulder, urging me forward, and Dree held the door for us.

Bree lowered her arm and grasped my hand as she led us to the back of the bar and patted a seat for me to sit in. I hung my jacket on the back and slung my purse on the purse hook in front of it, then slid onto the seat and crossed my legs, loving the way my stockinged legs slid against each other as I tugged my miniskirt under me.

Dree sat to my right and Bree to my left. They swiveled their seats and Bree's stockinged leg rested against mine, as did Dree's jeaned leg. His hand nonchalantly landed on my thigh and squeezed it as he leaned into my face, his eyes bright. "Their charcuterie board is the best. Wasabi nuts, candied pecans, meats, cheeses, even has anchovies."

I placed my hand on his, not wanting it to leave my leg. "I can't wait. Thanks so much for stopping and having me join you two."

I squeezed his hand affectionately and glided it on my thigh, then let it go, hoping he'd keep gliding it. He did and sat back in his seat, looking at the menu. I was in heaven and throbbing in my panties, loving his sweet caresses.

Bree's soft, silky hand landed on my knee below Dree's hand and she slid it around. "Love that you're wearing stockings. Few girls do these days. I *love* wearing them. They add a delicate finishing touch and the sensation of them on the skin is so lovely... aren't they wonderful?"

I nodded and smiled nervously as she slid her hand around on my knee and Dree caressed my thigh, and my happy little girl under my skirt leapt and jumped beneath it.

"Dree loves them too, as you can tell. I can always count on him caressing my legs all night. Hope you like that. If not, tell him no and I'll switch seats with you. Right, Dree?"

He laughed and looked up from the menu. "I guess I have a thing for them... especially on beautiful women." He gave a very cute, crooked smile and winked.

I patted his thigh. "You can do that all night, Dree. Unless Bree gets jealous."

She shook her head. "He deserves some new legs to touch. We're old buddies."

The bartender came over and smiled at me. I looked at the drink menu and pointed with my glossy painted nail. "I'll have the bourbon flower martini."

"Good choice. Intense leather and wood with a touch of sweet lavender." He turned to Bree.

"Hi Joey. Dree and I will have our usual drinks, right Dree?" He nodded. "Dirty is good."

She nodded. "And how about 18 oysters? Put all of it on my tab. I'm welcoming a new person to the neighborhood. Lee, this is Joey. Joey, Lee."

"Hi! Nice to meet you, Joey." I extended a hand and shook his with my fingertips.

"And a pleasure to meet you, pretty lady. I hope you enjoy our neighborhood. I'll put the order in and get those drinks going." He winked.

"Bree. That was so nice of you. Thank you for buying all that. Next stuff is on my tab."

She smiled, nodded and leaned in, putting her long-painted-nail fingers under my chin and gave me a peck on the lips. "You're welcome. So happy to find a new friend." Both her hands caressed my knees as she gazed into my eyes. "I think we'll be excellent friends."

I nodded. "I think we will."

She leaned back and stretched her arms, looking around. Dree put all the menus into a pile to the side of him and continued nonchalantly caressing my thigh.

I was relaxed and so thankful to have found these two on my first day being me. My body tingled, my pretty girl in my panties oozed. I sipped the water through my straw, my painted fake nails glinting in the light as they delicately and femininely held it.

The only thing that could go wrong right now is if I was overwhelmed with all the sensuality and caressing from Dree and wet my panties and skirt, giving away my secret. I didn't want him to stop, so I just endured the sweet torture and held back as well as I could. I bounced a crossed leg.

Our drinks arrived. My frosted martini was a gorgeous golden color with an edible flower floating on the top and the rim dipped in lemon sugar. I held the stem, my nails and rings glinting in the drop-light of the bar. I cautiously lifted it and looked at Bree and Dree. "To good friends and happy times."

They both repeated the phrase, and we delicately touched rims and sipped.

My eyes popped wide. "Mmm, a Bourbon Flower. Very intense. Lovely. Wood, leather, flowers. It even smells pretty." I licked a taste of the rim, then sipped more.

Bree nodded. "A favorite of mine, too. Into salt and savory tonight."

The oysters came and Joey put plates before us so we could serve ourselves from the iced bowl of them. They were delectable and minerally and luscious.

Dree was busy with both hands, and I got a break from the arousing touches. Bree touched my hand. "So, Lee. What brings you here?"

I told her about my decision.

"Really? I'm in the last year of Nuke too. Dree is Mechanical." Her hand slid under the bar to my thigh and took over from Dree. Gazing into her made-up eyes and her touch made me throb once more. She was seductive as hell.

"Cool! How weird."

Bree's hand drifted higher and her fingers slid between my thighs. I clenched them tightly. She slid them out and began gliding them back and forth. "So, Lee. What else can you tell us about yourself? Any boyfriends? Girlfriends? Any plans for the future?"

I sipped the rest of my martini and moved it to the edge of the bar so Joey could see I wanted another. "Hmm, no. No. And make money. Someone to love would be nice. As you know. Not much time for relationships in engineering school, but after... after I hope to have someone to love."

Dree pushed his martini to the edge. "Want a family?"

"Eh. Not really. I *should*... You know... It's *expected*. My dad would want that. He wanted the ideal..." I looked around. "Uh kid."

"I see. My dad thinks I'm a no good faggot. He thinks I'm too fem to be his son."

"I kinda have the same situation."

Oops. I slipped. TMI. My skin flushed. My drink arrived, and I lifted it.

"Good friends and happy times." I sipped. "So. How about you guys? What's your story? Gonna get married to each other?"

Dree laughed and looked at Bree. "I wouldn't mind living with Bree forever. She's my best friend. I don't think she's ready to commit, though, and I'm not really either. Who knows what will happen after college, right?"

I nodded.

Dree nodded. "So your dad thought you weren't the ideal daughter, huh? Like I wasn't the ideal son. Sounds like we have more in common. Bree had a similar issue too. Conservative parents suck, but we all became adults, and it doesn't matter anymore."

"Right." I sipped. I had guilt from hiding something. Even though Dree was still caressing me, I was no longer aroused. I looked over to Bree, who was people watching and relaxing, her gorgeous legs crossed and bouncing a foot in her high heels. They were very likeable. They thought I was a girl. They deserved the truth.

"Uh... Bree? Dree?"

I looked at each of them. An obvious look of concern on my face. Bree leaned in toward me and moved a curl from my face. "What's the matter, princess? You look frightened."

"Uh... I'm lying and I hate that."

"That's okay. We forgive you. What are you lying about?"

"I'm uh... I'm... Not a girl. There. I said it."

Bree made a face. Dree scoffed. I blew it. It didn't know I did, but their faces showed disgust. "I'm so sorry."

Dree squeezed my thigh. "Don't be sorry. You *are* a girl. *All* girl. It's not what's *under* your skirt that determines that, it's how you feel and what's in your head." He smiled and tapped my forehead with his finger.

"Ouch!"

"Sorry."

Bree gave me a hug and kissed my cheek. "You're *all* girl, honey. I know. I'm all girl too and I know a girl when I see one." She looked around the bar. No one was near, and we were at the back. Taking my hand, she opened my fingers, then placed it on her thigh. She looked deep into my eyes and slid my hand under her skirt to her panties. She slid the panties aside and wrapped my fingers around a thick, long, hard cock.

My eyes burst open. She laughed and took her hand away. I squeezed it. "That's it. Make sure it's real. Stroke it for me, Lee." She looked around while I did. I didn't want to let it go.

My mind raced. I had found a girl like me and I'd never have guessed it. She leaned in and kissed me deeply on the lips, then put her hand on my head and wrapped her fingers in my curls and whispered to me. "Your hand is so soft, and it's touch is heavenly. You can do that anytime, Lee. You have the *touch* of a girl. So sensual."

I sniffed her perfume in her hair, and my other hand caressed her stockinged thigh. Uncontrollably throbbing in my panties, my heart raced. I stroked her faster and faster, wanting to make her feel wonderful. It was thrilling holding someone else's cock for the first time. I had to stop jerking her off, or mine would spurt. I withdrew my hand and looked around. Joey smiled at the other end of the bar and nodded.

I leaned back, took a deep breath, and sipped my drink. Dree slapped my thigh. "There. Now you can relax. Your secret was no big deal."

I observed Dree. He was being sincere. I could sense it. Long eyelashes revealed his mascara. My eyes flitted around him, taking in everything about him now. There was a fine line of eyeliner at the base of the lashes I hadn't noticed before. He lifted his hand, and I noticed the light glint off the clear nail polish on his finely manicured, slightly long nails. Was he like me, too? His button down black shirt was pressed neatly, as were his jeans. His boots were polished and had three-inch heels. He had that pretty face and thick, wavy hair to his shoulders, which, when it revealed his ears, showed three piercing holes in each ear like I have. Only one hole in each ear held a stud in them tonight.

"Dree? Thank you!" I looked at Bree, then back at Dree. Thank you both. I'm honored you shared that with me and happy I told you both.

Joey came over and checked on us. "Doing okay ladies? Uh, Dree?"

Bree ordered a charcuterie tray and another round of drinks.

"On my tab Joey. Please?"

"Sure, sweetheart. If it's okay with Bree and Dree."

They nodded. "Sure. Let her have it this time. Don't want to make her feel bad." She rubbed my thigh and pressed her fingers between my crossed legs. I lifted one slightly, and she slid it up to my panties and pressed on my hardness while she smiled at Joey. Joey winked and left.

I opened my legs. Bree slid my panties aside and wrapped her cool, soft fingers around it and stroked me, one arm around my shoulder, her breath warm in my ear. "Mmm, very nice, girl. It's very, very nice. So velvety, so hard." Her finger tip rubbed the tip and made me shudder. "And it's oozing. Mmm."

"Uh... better stop that... Please? It's too much right now. I have a hair trigger."

She pulled back and grinned. "Nice. I like that. Glad you're feeling so sexy and pretty tonight."

"Me too. It can be a little much, though. This is the first time I've gone out in public fully dressed like this. You know. As a girl. It's all so sensual."

"I know it is, isn't it? I've gotten used to it and it isn't so constant anymore. It still feels nice... Much better than jeans and boots." She looked at Dree and shook her head.

Drinks arrived, and we all clinked and sipped. Bree motioned to Dree with her drink. "Dree there. She seems to think it's better when she dresses like a guy for a while. Then when she's a girl, it's more intense for her."

Dree nodded, smiling. "Yup. You're right, Lee. Me too. I'm a girl too. A girl playing a guy right now. Joey knows both of me. That's why he called us ladies, then paused and corrected it for you, because I'm a guy tonight. Kinda. A girl in guys' clothes." He laughed.

Our charcuterie board arrived, and we munched and drank and talked about their experiences and how we got to where we were and it was all incredible. We were like old friends, all relaxed and touchy feely. I'd rub Dree's crotch, jerk Bree under her skirt, she'd stroke me under mine. I even got Dree's package out all the way and stroked him while I chatted with Joey.

It was so weird and yet so natural. At least the drinks had somewhat dampened my desire to the point I didn't have to worry about coming spontaneously and could just enjoy the sensuality of everything. I was falling in love with my new life and my new friends.

I stretched and yawned. I found the clock in the bar. It was midnight. We had been there for seven hours already. I forced my eyes open. I heard myself in my girly voice. "Oh... My... God... It's midnight."

Bree stroked me and looked into my eyes. "So... will you turn into a pumpkin now?"

"No, but. I mean. I usually go to sleep at ten and get up at six. It's been a long day."

"We normally do too, but... It's summer break and we don't have school or work tomorrow. We both don't start for two weeks."

"Oh god. I have to find a job too. Well, I don't need one really, but I can't not work."

"You'll get one. Don't worry." She looked around. "Yeah, we should probably go. Nothing good ever happens late at night in bars. Where do you live? Did you drive?"

"Walked. Just on Chester around the corner and down the street."

"We're on Chester too. We'll all walk home together then and we can see where we all live and while we're walking, plan something to do tomorrow if you want. Right Dree?"

Dree nodded, his eyelids drooping. He sipped his beer.

I finished my beer, stood, adjusted my skirt, and put on my crop denim jacket. They stood, and we said goodbye to Joey, leaving a big tip and walked out the door and down the sidewalk arm in arm.

The fresh air was invigorating and the full moon lit the Victorian flower beds in front of the houses as we approached my house. "It's right there." I pointed.

Bree shook her head. Chuckled. "We're two down from you." She pointed. "Dree is my roomie." She snuggled next to me. "Mm, it's nice to be close to you like this." She pulled Dree to her. "You too, sleepyhead."

We made our way to the front porch, and I dug in my purse for the key. "Come in and have a beer? Lemonade?"

"Lemonade sounds great. Dree could use it too. She'll be better for it in the morning."

Dree nodded.

I opened the door and let them in, then stepped past them to lead them to the kitchen. I poured three lemonades, and we took them into the parlor. Dree slugged his down, put it on the end table and fell onto the couch.

Bree led me to the love seat, and we both sat and crossed our legs. We sipped our tea. I could sense her nervousness and I was uneasy as well. What should we do? Would she want to? Should we? Is it too late? Should I walk Bree home?

I looked over at Dree. I motioned to him. He was sound asleep. "He can sleep there if you think he'll be comfortable."

"That's fine. He'll be out all night now." Bree gazed lovingly at me. Her reddish hair and darker skin were stunning, as were her makeup and presentation. "So, are you Irish at all? Your hair... but your skin..."

"A mix. The hair is from the Irish, my mom. The skin and cheekbones are from my dad. Half American Indian, half black as night African. He was tall and my mom was tinier than me. Maybe that's why I really like a tall black man now and then." She laughed and rubbed my thigh, gazing at me. "What are you?"

"Boring. English. They came over on the Mayflower. I'm sure a lot of stuff has mixed in since then, though."

"You look so tired. Would it be bad of me to ask if I can take you to bed upstairs? I don't have a cat or anything I need to go home for, and I'd like to be with you."

I stared at her drowsily. Was this for real? I sipped my lemonade.

4

She stood and took me by the hand. I nodded, and she helped me up the stairs to the bedroom. She pulled back the satin sheets, and I fell onto the bed and slid up to the pillow. She slid onto the other side.

My heart was racing, and I was wide awake. Bree's eyes were like beacons in the moonlight as it fell on her face. I slid over to her. She popped the snaps on my miniskirt and pulled it away, then undid hers and slid it off. She took off her panties and slid mine down and over my heels.

I slid my stockinged leg over her silky stockinged leg and humped my hardness against it, slipping and sliding while she did the same and we embraced and kissed. Our breasts crushed against each other's and our perfume mingled. We kissed and humped slowly, deliciously, our stockinged legs slipping against each other, our cocks gliding softly on our silken legs.

Bree reached around and grabbed our panties. She reached between us, wrapped our cocks in them, and held them against each other and we humped against each other's cocks. It amazed me how good it was to have another cock against mine. She was so hard and so velvety.

Her breathing got choppy, and she broke the kiss to look into my eyes. She stroked my hair. "Such a pretty girl you are."

"Oh god... So are you, Bree. It's like a dream." Vigorously, I humped harder into her panty covered hand against her cock. I whimpered and slid my legs against hers and squeezed her breast. I moved her hair from her face and looked into her eyes. "Huh... Oh god it's so deliscious against mine." I humped harder and faster. She held us loosely, sensually, touching cock to cock.

"That's it, little girl. Come against me. Come in our panties so we don't mess the bed. I'll come when you do."

Her eyes were intense. She bit her lip, her teeth gleaming in the moonlight. I whimpered and whined. I heard myself squeal as she embraced me and held us tight in her hand of panties. "That's it, little girl. Let it go for me. I will too. I need to." She humped her cock against mine. Her perfume wafted to my nose. I nuzzled her neck and kissed it.

I slid my legs against hers and humped hard and fast like an adolescent into a pillow and came like a rocket. Bree whimpered and squealed. I gasped and squeaked, my body shuddering. Her stockinged legs tensed and slid against mine. We both humped our cocks together, and she came in a flood over my cock and into the panties and our cream merged and soaked our swollen sexes.

We held each other tight, her grip loosened, and we both wet-humped against each other a few more times, slowing until we collapsed against each other. I peppered her face with kisses; her smile shining in the moonlight, her hand stroking my hair. "My lovely, lovely girl."

5

Birds chirped outside the window. Bree lay sleeping on her back next to me, a tent made of the satin sheet between her legs. I stared at it. I had never even touched a cock of anyone else, yet last night I touched two besides mine and I came against one. Now I had an addiction to other cocks. It twitched beneath the sheet. It twitched again and Bree rolled her head and let out a little moan.

I carefully pulled the sheet back, revealing a perfectly shaved, smooth hairless package, the shaft hard and begging for release. My morning wood was no less prominent as I slid over and gently took hers between my fingers, then licked the tip and took as much of it into my hot mouth that I could. Bree let out a moan and her hand rested on my head. She moved her hips to hump it into my face slowly while she twirled her fingers in my hair. I went nuts on it, running my tongue in circles around it, and bobbing my head, tugging and rolling her silky globes while I looked up at her face.

Her eyes popped open, and she smiled broadly. She gently took my head and slid me off her cock, then slid around on her side and took my cock into her mouth. I took hers back into mine and we began a dance of mutual indulgence. We got into time together, running circles, bobbing, sucking, tugging, rolling. Our hips moved in time, fucking each other's faces while we ministered to our delectables in our mouths.

Cock-muffled whimpers ensued from each of us and our legs tensed as we both approached the precipice. I held it back, and I thought she was doing the same until the point she gushed her cream into my mouth and I gulped it down. My body shuddered, and I gushed my passion into her face. We came together, our bodies shuddering and spasming, our cocks pulsing in each other's hot mouth while we both gulped and struggled to swallow it all. Soon, the pulses became dry, yet we tortured each other—flicking the head and tip with our tongues, making us both gasp and jerk and struggle.

We whimpered muted whimpers and forced each other to take those overwhelming electric jolts going through our bodies from flicking the now overly sensitive head and tip of the shaft.

Bree grasped my head tight and yanked her dick from my face. "Stop!" She laughed. "Oh, my god! I thought I could have you make me stop first but... Yeesh, girl!" She sat up against the backboard, her legs crossed in her stockings and heels. "Fuck! You're a very determined little girl." She laughed again and held her arms out. I moved over to her, and we hugged and embraced.

I ran my hand through her hair and kissed her neck. "Mmm, I like intense things. You're intense."

"Mmm, you too, sweetie. That was incredible."

"It was my first time. I never touched another cock until last night."

"Wow. I don't even know if I remember when I did. It must have been really special for you."

"It was. I'll never forget it. Ever." I gave her a peck on the lips. "Hungry?"

"You bet."

We slipped into fresh panties I took from the drawer and slid into our skirts, then descended the stairs. Dree was by the stove. He turned to us. "Morning ladies. French toast and bacon? Lee, I hope you don't mind that I ransacked your fridge."

"Not at all. Thanks for making breakfast. Sleep okay on the couch?"

He nodded and turned to the stove. "Yup. Like a baby. Feel like a million bucks. Thanks for the lemonade. I think that helped. Had to pee in the early morning though and didn't know where the bathroom was, so I hope you don't mind, I went out back behind the garage. The moon gave plenty of light to find my way, and no one could see me from there."

"No problem." I patted his shoulder, poured a coffee, and sat at the table with Bree. "So Dree. When do I get to see the real you? The pretty, feminine, sexy you."

"Since you asked, anytime."

"Today? Three girls relaxing? Shopping? Sitting in cafes? Walking in parks? Whatever."

"Sure. We'll need to go home and change, of course."

"I have plenty of clothes if you two want to try some of mine. I just filled the wardrobe yesterday and they're all brand new."

Dree placed the plates of French toast before us and sat down. "That sounds great, but we need to shower and clean out. Do you have an attachment for your shower?"

"Attachment?"

"Yeah. So after you poop you can clean out your butt, so it's fresh and clean if it needs to be used. All us girls do that. Don't want a mess. I'd think you'd know that."

"Uh... I never thought of having anything in my butt. Not an attachment or even something else. Eww!"

Bree took my hand and looked at me. "Honey. You have to. It's part of the experience of being a girl. You can't imagine how good it is to be filled up down there and made love to. It's very *full-filling* if you get my drift. You really are a virgin, aren't you?"

My face flushed. I nodded and ate.

"Don't be embarrassed. You'll learn. We'll teach you. Pick out your clothes, come over, and you can use our shower, and after, we'll get you an attachment today and install it."

"But... My butt... I don't want that."

"Trust me. You will. You never had cocks in your hand or mouth either, and now look at you. Break your paradigm. We'll even gift you a toy today to get you started."

"A toy?"

"A very pleasant girl's toy. Yes. A reward for cleaning out."

I rolled my head. "Oh god. Here we go. Okay."

Dree laughed and chewed. "So, did you girls sleep well? Did you not sleep well too?"

Bree scoffed. "If you must know, nosey, yes. Last night we frotted. This morning we sixty-nined. It was wonderful. Right Lee?"

"Incredible."

Dree nodded, looking at us both and grinning. "I knew it. That's good to hear, though. I'm happy for you both. I just regret falling asleep last night and waking up on a couch with a woodie this morning and no one around." He looked up in the air and rolled his eyes, grinning. "I *still* have it."

Bree and I looked at each other. I shrugged my shoulders. Bree smiled and looked at Dree. "Okay. If you're going to be good and become a pretty girl like you should, Dree, and if we deem you deserving of it, then to get everyone on the same page today, after we all get cleaned up and dressed, Lee and I will take care of poor little Dree's annoying little hard-on so she can pay attention to something other than her dick today. Right Lee?"

I nodded. "Sounds nice. If she's a good girl and she becomes the girl she's meant to be, and she promises to stop masquerading as a male for *at least* the next few days."

Dree raised her eyebrows. "*Few days*? It'll be old and boring by then."

I scrunched my eyebrows at him. "It won't. We'll keep it new and fresh for you. Besides. Isn't it boring masquerading as a guy?"

He shrugged. "Somewhat. It is less work, but being a girl every day is like eating brownies every day. You don't appreciate them as much. Heck, I guess I could do it for two lovely ladies like you two though... *And* that *BJ* from both of you this morning, after we're dressed, of course. Deal."

Bree looked confused. "Who said BJ? We haven't determined what would be proper for you yet. You still might have to jerk off into some panties."

Dree let out a long sigh. "Whatever." His hand slid between his legs and he started rubbing himself through his pants as he ate. He grinned at us both.

Bree scolded. "Not now, young lady!" She laughed.

6

I enjoyed a coffee on the patio, took my morning dump, cleaned up the house a little, then packed a little bag with my clothes and shoes and things for the day and walked down the street to their house. Bree and Dree were both finished showering, and I slid into their bathroom and got into the shower. I ran a quick blade across my body and washed my hair and conditioned it. I stared at the attachment as if it were an alien probe.

With the lever turned, the water redirected through the attachment. Hmm. I used it like they told me to. It was a strange sensation, but not totally unpleasant. After a couple of minutes, it was done. I washed my body and got out of the shower.

Hair fluffed and dried and looking lovely framing my face, I did my makeup and sat down and slid on my cut-out-gusset, sheer suntan pantyhose. I slid on the pink silky panties and put on a matching bra, then filled it with my forms and adjusted my cleavage. I slid into a beige, flower printed, cap sleeve, cotton V-neck minidress, then fastened my matching wedge heels on my ankles and stood.

I checked myself in the full-length mirror on the back of the door. Lovely! The dress was flirty and very thin and light and perfect for a summer day. I sprayed perfume all over and put in my long dangle earrings and put on my necklace and rings, then headed downstairs to the patio where Bree and Dree were.

Dree looked incredible as a girl and she wore a short jumper skirt, revealing her shapely legs and creamy cleavage. Her makeup made her pretty face pop as she beamed at me while I walked toward them across the pavers. "My Dree! You *should* be a girl *all* the time. You're so pretty."

She ran her long fake nailed fingers across herself, then held her arms out in a display of herself and nodded. "Thank you! It's very nice to be her again. Now, about my situation." She rubbed her crotch through her skirt. "It hasn't gone away." She grinned. "I need to catch up with you two."

Bree nodded and put her iced tea down. She looked around and found two pillows and tossed them before Dree. She took my hand and led us to Dree and had her stand up. We knelt down before her.

Bree lifted Dree's skirt and tucked it out of the way, then pulled aside Dree's skorts and panties and revealed her begging package. We both worked at it fervently.

Dree had a hand on each of our heads, looking down at us, looking up. She was so pretty. When it was my turn to suck her, I did my best to outdo Bree and made Dree whimper, and bite her lower lip and squeeze my head.

Dree sat back on her haunches and let me have at it while she watched. "Go ahead, girl. Milk her."

I mumbled around the shaft and continued to drive Dree crazy. I could tell she was ready if I'd only let her, but I was enjoying it too much to let her. I dragged it out for her, bringing her to the edge repeatedly until it was too much for me to take. I was afraid I was going to wet my panties if I indulged in Dree's arousal and torture any further.

I brought her to full rigid and sucked the come from her while looking into her eyes, her knees weak as she shot gush after gush into my face. I nearly came myself, her passion for me was so great. When she finished delivering the cream, I continued on until she yanked me off her and tucked it all away.

"Wow. You are persistent, girl. You could have just finished me quickly too, but the torture was pretty nice. You definitely look very sexy with it stuffed in your pretty face and I could have made my deposit as soon as it was stuffed into it." She laughed and sat back down while Bree and I went back to our seats.

Bree crossed her legs and checked her purse. "Well, what shall we do today, ladies? Dree, I think first we have a little thing we have to do for Lee before we leave. While she's all horny from sucking you."

"Oh yeah. Right. I put the new one in my purse because I didn't know when we were gonna do it."

I raised my eyebrows. "Do what?"

Dree grinned. "You cleaned out like we asked you to, right?" I nodded.

"Good. Then get on the ground one more time, but this time on your knees and put your butt in the air and your face on your arms on the ground."

"Oh, no."

Bree pushed me. "Oh yes. You have to. It'll open up a whole new world for you. Now do it. Get down there."

I took those pillows and knelt on one and put the other in front of me and lowered my head onto my arms on it. I tried to look back at them as Dree lifted my dress.

Bree pulled my panties aside and grabbed my now softening shaft. "This won't do. It needs to be hard in order to open the door or you'll clench and it'll hurt." She released my package and milked me like a cow from underneath. It didn't take long to harden, and I humped into her soft hand automatically while looking back at her. "Mmm, that's really nice, Bree. I've never been milked like a cow before. It's really erotic."

"Good." She nodded to Dree behind me. Dree moved my panties to the side and something wet and cold slid between my butt cheeks.

I gasped. "Uh oh. Go slow."

She did, and it pressed against my tight hole. Bree continued jerking me. The sensation on my hole was erotic, and I pressed against it needing more. Dree pressed some more. Before I knew it, it had slid in and stopped at the hilt. I heard a pumping sound, and it swelled inside of me. "Wow. Huh..."

Dree said, "Tell me when you're *full-filled*." Shew chuckled.

"Huh, huh... Uh.... Oh god, yes. It's stretching me. I'm so full. That's good. Stop."

I gasped and humped into Bree's hand while I whimpered. Bree let me go.

"Hey. That was incredible. Don't stop. Let me finish."

"No. Not now. You need to stay that way all day so you'll be begging for more later. Don't worry, you won't be alone. I'm wearing one right now too, as is Dree. Stand up and tuck yourself in."

I did, and Bree took her phone out. She tapped the face with her nails. "I sent you an app. Download it and put it on your phone, then open it and pair it with the plug."

I did as instructed and soon the plug was sending silent vibrations into me, making me ooze in my panties. I adjusted it lower, so it was just pleasant and didn't drive me crazy. Just a little crazy, maybe. I laughed. "Incredible. It's so nice. I never would have guessed."

I walked around the patio. The sensation of the plug filling me and the vibrations added a swing to my hips, and it made me feel so feminine and girly it was wonderful. I couldn't stop smiling. I slung my purse over my shoulder. "Okay, where to? If you both have one in like I do, I'd think you'd want to walk for sure."

Dree grinned and nodded and put her hand on my shoulder. "For sure. How about a walk across town to a bistro for lunch?"

We walked, the three of us hand in hand, our breasts jiggling, plugs running, hips swaying, and I'm sure even Dree had her panties full of hard, sensual shaft, throbbing inside of them. This was going to be one heck of a day.

7

I never enjoyed walking so much. It was a beautiful day, and we stayed in the residential area until it was time to cut over to the commercial area. The air was sweet with the smells of fresh cut grass and flowers. The breeze flitted with the hem of my minidress and caressed my stockinged legs. My breasts jiggled and tugged deliciously on my chest. My hips swayed, and the plug fired off from time to time, sending ripples of pleasure into me, making my pantied pet girl throb. It was a total sensual delight, and I was at the edge of release through the whole time.

We chatted while we walked, and Bree and Dree spoke of their various escapades with various men, femboys, and other girls like us. This further contributed to our arousal as we journeyed to the bistro.

We arrived just in time for lunch. Bree led us onto the shaded patio and found us three seats at a table overlooking the rest of the place from an elevated section. It was good to sit. Walking in high-heeled wedges isn't difficult, but walking for that long made my calves tired. Not to mention all the arousal took some energy as well.

We perused the menus and ordered a light lunch and iced teas. I sat, slipping the hem of my dress under my thighs, and leaned back in my chair, crossed my legs, and observed the arriving lunch customers. I bounced one high-heeled foot, indulging in the sensuality of my stockinged legs against each other and all the rest of my newfound, incredible femininity.

Dree poked Bree and leaned in toward her. "Is that them?"

Bree nodded and smiled broadly. "Oh yeah. It sure is. They must have another conference on campus this year."

I touched Bree's hand. "Who are they? Should we leave?"

"Hell no. When they see us, we're guaranteed the best sex of our lives, honey. We met them last year. They come over from Uganda to raise money and politic with other nations to support LGBTQ rights in Uganda. It's a mess over there. Right now, it's the death penalty to be gay."

"Wow. That sucks. So you met them last year?"

"Sure did. They're all over six feet tall and they all seem to fulfill the tales of black men and the size of their meat. I never saw any as big as theirs. Wait until you have one of *those* shooting inside of you, girl. It taught me why my mom liked black men so much." She laughed.

I watched the men in their summer suits looking handsome and professional as they sat at their table. They groomed themselves well. Thinking about what Bree said made me nervous. There I was sitting on a pumped up plug that vibrated inside of me on and off, my body at attention and aroused, yet the thought of being ripped apart by a big black man was scary. But now I knew how good something in me could be, and even if I didn't do that, I sure could imagine sucking on one like that.

Our iced tea and food arrived, and we started eating. Bree and Dree looked over at the men on and off. I couldn't help it either. When the men laughed and smiled, their eyes lit up and their teeth flashed their joyous smiles. Being LGBTQ rights people and having already done Bree and Dree last year, there was no need to worry about our secrets. The more I watched the exotic-looking men, the more I wanted to get to know them better.

We paid our check and stood to go to the ladies' room, then leave. Bree led us past the men's table on the way. They recognized her as she approached and smiles filled their faces. They all stood and came away from the table. "Bree, Dree!"

One of them put his arms out and hugged her and another hugged Dree and they exchanged greetings until they were all done and then a large hand flung out to me. I took it and shook it with my fingertips. "Hi!"

"Hello, my name is Akello. This is Dembe, and this is Bale."

Each nodded and smiled broadly, then offered their hand. I shook each gently, looking up into their eyes as they bowed and nodded, shaking my hand. They were breathtaking. They smelled of some sort of fresh cologne. Akello waved the waiter over for their bill and paid it while Bree and Dembe caught up.

Dembe asked Bree. "Would you ladies be free for dinner tonight? If you are, we'd be honored if we could take you to dinner someplace nice."

Bree nodded quickly, excited as a little girl. "Oh god yes. That would be lovely. I can make reservations for us and we can meet there. Same place as last year?"

"That would be fabulous. We'd all be very grateful. Rather than meet there, how about we pick you up at six?"

"Perfect. I'll text my address. Same phone?"

"Yes. Can we give you a lift somewhere? We're going back to the campus to finish the conference." He looked at his watch. "If there is somewhere on the way, or if you'd like to go to campus with us, we can give you a ride. Our driver is out front."

Bree looked at us. "I think the campus would be fine. It gets us close to home and then we can walk anywhere from there easily. We haven't decided what we're doing this afternoon yet."

"Perfect. May I?" Dembe offered his arm. Bree took it. Akello offered his to me and Bale to Dree, and we all left on their arms. The Limo pulled in front and the driver held the door for us. We slid into the back—Bree, Dembe, me, Akello, Dree, then Bale.

Us girls slid the hems of our minidresses under us and crossed our legs in the huge limo. The six of us fit nicely on the L-shaped seat. I clasped my hands and rested them on my knee while taking it all in. Akello's hard thigh rested against mine. He was built like a rock, yet not incredibly wide. Tall, firm, handsome.

I glanced down at his crotch and could see the outline in his beige dress pants of a substantial tool that wasn't even hard, as it wrapped like a snake in a curve on his leg. His arm drapped over my shoulder. "I hope you don't mind my arm. It's just more comfortable to stretch it out. You're a beautiful lady, by the way, if I may say so. I don't want to be impolite." He smiled.

I turned my head to look up at him and leaned into his powerful arm. "Not impolite at all. Very kind of you to give me that compliment. *You're* very *handsome,* if I may say so."

"Thank you, young lady." He looked out the window. "It's wonderful here where people can be who they are. I wish someday for our country to become so free."

"It does sound horrible in Uganda. The death penalty for being gay. It's horrendous."

He nodded. "Certainly is. Well, hopefully our trip will be beneficial." I glanced down quickly at his crotch and noticed the snake had straightened out some, but wasn't fully erect yet. It was substantial. I got stuck staring at it. Akello laughed. I turned to look outside quickly and felt my face flush, having been caught.

"Don't worry. You pay me a compliment by staring like you did." He whispered in my ear, "You may touch it if you like."

My heart raced. I looked at his smiling face and looked around the car at the others in conversation. No one would notice. I slid my hand across his thigh and placed my palm on it. I grasped it through the fabric. It throbbed for me and I gazed into his deep, dark, smiling eyes. I throbbed in my panties. The plug fired off. I took my hand away and recrossed my legs, played with my hair.

He whispered. "Nice?"

I nodded nervously.

"Thank you. Maybe this evening we'll have more time to explore. If you're interested."

My head down and eyes up, I nodded quickly. Took a deep breath and recrossed my legs and unconsciously caressed them.

He grinned. "Don't be so nervous, sweet girl. Relax." He looked out the window. "Ah, we're there. See you tonight?"

I nodded.

"Wonderful."

I couldn't resist another look at his crotch. It was solid and huge. I smiled a crooked smile, and he winked at me and chuckled before we got out.

8

The Limo pulled away as the men walked off toward the conference. We stood there watching them. Bree took my arm and hugged it to her. "So little girl. I saw you checking out Akello's manhood. Nice, huh?"

I rolled my eyes. "Oh, my god. I never would have believed it. I'm afraid he'll rip me in two."

She laughed. "You'd be surprised how far we can stretch when we want to. You'll be fine. Now, the restaurant is a classy place. Do you have a nice dress for it?"

"Nothing really fancy. I mostly bought college type clothes. You know. Less formal and more casual. Like this dress and the denim skirt I wore before."

"Then we need to pick up a dress for you. You need to be ready for your first time having love made to you. It's like your prom night, girl!" She turned to Dree. "Dree. We're taking our virgin Bree shopping for a new dress to get laid in for the first time."

The three of us walked hand in hand across campus and down to a formal shop where the girls picked out a black, corseted top and sequined-layered minidress. It fit beautifully and didn't need a bra and the gel breast forms tucked in, giving perfect cleavage. A matching black sequined bolero came with it and we found matching strappy stilettos with five-inch heels. I bought matching costume jewelry, a purse, a hairpiece, crotchless panties, garter belt and sheer black lace top stockings.

Bree and Dree found fresh dresses for themselves as well, and we all checked out. We each carried our dress bags and a side bag of things out of the store.

I checked my watch. "Should we Uber? I'd like to save some energy and time if anyone's interested."

They both nodded. Bree laughed. "Good idea, Lee."

Back home, I unpacked my things and placed them on the bed. I removed the plug, washed it and put it away, took a bath, ran a quick razor over things and loofahed my body.

Silky scented skin lotion sealed my skin in silk. I fluffed and sprayed my hair, working the fine strands of bling I bought to match the dress into my curls. I redid my makeup for a dramatic evening look and applied twenty-four-hour, suck-proof lipstick, twitching at the thought of his manly shaft in my lips.

I stepped into the bedroom, my little girl at attention, dancing with each step. Sitting on the bed, I wrapped the black lace garter belt around my waist, fastened it and straightened it, then slid the gossamer thin, black lace top stockings up, giving me a shiver of delight. My pretty painted toenails gleamed from under the sheer fabric.

Loosening the corset top, I wiggled into the dress, put my arms through the thin straps and tugged the corset strings snug. Inserting the gel breast forms, I adjusted them and tightened the corset top further, snugging them up and making cleavage, then tightened the waist strands, cinching my waist tight, flat and narrow. The sequined layered skirt of the dress fluffed nicely about my thighs, just long enough to hide the tops of my stockings.

I slid up the new crotchless panties that framed my happy little rigid girl in a nest of ruffles and lace while she danced in the air. Silver garters with bows then slid up my legs to rest over the clasps of the garter belt. Fluffing the skirt down, I could see there was no sign of my little girl's incredible arousal beneath it all.

I took a soft, black satin ribbon from the bed and tied it over the shaft and under my globes and snugged it, lifting the package up and out. I wrapped it one more time around the globes beneath and then again over the shaft and under the globes. Tying a bow, I arranged it neatly. The arrangement further feminized my little girl in the nest and held her proudly out and up. Taking the twenty-four-hour lipstick, I carefully painted the head of it to match my lips. I blew on it to dry it and watched it leap up and down a few times before covering it up with the dress.

The fetishy tall, strappy stilettos secured firmly about my feet with the three ankle straps. Silver dangle ankle bracelets graced the curve of my delicate ankle in their bondage. Stepping in tiny steps to the dresser, I put in the three dangling, fake diamond, pierced earrings in each ear. The necklace rested in my cleavage, drawing the eye there. Bracelets slid onto my wrists. Rings bejeweled my fingers, their long painted nails glinting in the light. I loaded my purse and hung it on my shoulder, then slung my thumb through to rest on it.

In a forced minced step from the fetishy tall shoes, I stepped over to the full-length mirror. I sprayed perfume over and under the dress, in my hair, on my neck and put myself in a cloud of feminine scent. I stared at myself in the mirror. Akello would be crazy for me. I was crazy for me.

My eyes flitted about my legs, delicate arms, shoulders, hair, and face. My hand had its own mind and found an alert girlfriend beneath my dress and was jerking her furiously while my breath became choppy and my knees became weak. I yanked my hand from her, straightened my dress, then adjusted my hair and the strands of bling in it.

I checked my watch. Plenty of time to stroll over to Dree's and Bree's. I looked at myself in the mirror one more time. I couldn't help bringing myself to the edge again, looking at myself and the little girl with the prettily painted, oozing tip as I jerked her to the edge three more times.

I folded the bolero jacket and hung it on my slung purse, then took a deep breath and carefully navigated the stairs to leave.

9

Stepping carefully off the porch, the breeze wafted under my dress, bathing my unfettered girl in coolness and kissing my arms and shoulders while fluttering my curls on them. My heels clicked an erotic tempo as I stepped quickly in a tiny, vulnerable stride, my breasts tugging on my chest. The fresh scent of mowed grass mingled with my perfume, creating a surrealness to the atmosphere. Each step, the silky fabric of the dress kissed my little oozing girl as I made my way.

I rang the bell and heard Bree call out from the window upstairs to go inside and have a drink and they'd be right down. Passing through the door, I shut it behind me, clicked into the kitchen, and opened the fridge to find a pitcher of dirty martinis. I poured one into the stemmed glasses on the counter.

I wondered if they too had an emergency pack of smokes and checked the drawer to find one and a lighter. I took them out with me to the patio and took a seat, crossing my legs and tucking my little girl into the fluff of my dress to bounce a foot, trapping her and making her happy.

Lighting the smoke, I relished the heightened alertness the nicotine gave me as my senses went into full receptiveness and my skin tingled all over. Relishing the beautiful day, my state of mind, and the loveliness of femininity, I relaxed in the shade and sipped and smoked.

The seductive sound of multiple high heels clicked in concert and gained volume as they approached across the porch and across the patio. Dree wore a light beige, flared-hem, minidress with choker neck and keyhole top, revealing cleavage and bare, delicate shoulders. She wore sheer suntan stockings, flat-soled, thin-strapped stilettos, her hair in loose pigtails on each side of her head up high. She looked so cute and sexy.

Bree walked behind her in a long bronze satin dress, her leg poking through the slit with each step, her breasts jiggling her revealed cleavage, and her reddish brown hair bouncing free and fluffy about her shoulders. There was an obvious bulge showing beneath her dress that said her little girl was thrilled and ready for fun. She was a vision.

They sat with their drinks and crossed their legs. They raised their drinks. Bree spoke in her honey voice, "To one *hell* of a girl's night out."

I raised mine and sipped. "So, Bree. I uh... I could see your arousal through your dress. It's amazing and very sexy, but are you planning on getting rid of it before we leave?"

"Hell no. Dembe asked me to wear a dress that would show it. He said that was as beautiful as the rest of us and we should all do that when we can."

"I see. Is the restaurant we're going to okay for that?"

She scoffed. "That's what my purse is for. I'll carry it over it when we walk in or go to the bathroom and so on. No one will know except Dembe and the rest of us. You and Dree should let it show too."

I shrugged. "It won't show in this dress and probably won't in Dree's, but it can be free and bounce around and be easy to get to like it is right now."

"True. Too late to change clothes now, right? Your girls' dresses are easier to wear and feel nicer, anyway. I just did this for Dembe." She sipped her drink, then checked her watch. "I see you found our emergency smokes. Nervous?"

"A little. More like over stimulated, so I wanted to get *more* stimulated and have a smoke if that makes any sense." I giggled and puffed the last puff, then stripped it and held it in my hand.

"Just toss it in the bushes. Keeps the bugs away," Dree said.

I tossed it.

Bree pounded her drink and stood, her hardness nearly poking out of the slit. She slung her purse cross body and maneuvered it to hide it. "There. Ready, ladies? They should be here any second."

We all stood, walked in, placed our glasses in the dishwasher and headed out to the front porch. The Limo pulled up as we reached the street. The driver ran around the car and opened the door for us. We climbed in the back with the men, who were spread out with seats next to them for us. Akello's arm hugged me to him. "You look stunning, young lady."

"Thank you. I love your stiff collared shirt and the bow tie and black suit. Very handsome and classy."

"Thank you."

I sniffed his shoulder. "And you smell incredible."

"We had time to freshen up, so I took a shower and shaved my body and made it fresh and clean for you."

"How nice." I squeezed his hard thigh as best I could with my hand. I took his hand and placed it on my leg and glided it on my stocking, then placed my palm on his crotch and rubbed it.

He moved my hand away. "Sorry. It isn't far to the place and I can't walk in with it at attention." He chuckled.

"Oops. Sorry. Couldn't resist."

"No problem."

I snuggled next to him, being safe and secure with his arm around me, his big hand gently enlivening my body through my stockinged leg. We chatted about Uganda and all the good things about it, so I'd have something other than the bad things to know it by. His accent was intoxicating as he spoke and put me further into a surreal realm while I gazed into those bright, dark, deep eyes, and he spoke passionately about his home.

The valet opened our doors, and they led us into a private room overlooking a garden with a round, eight person, which we fit into comfortably. We ordered drinks and chatted as a group, my hand now able to indulge in exploring Akello through his pants. He rewarded me with a full, although hidden, erection.

On our second drink with oysters and cracked crab, I tried to get his package out of his pants, but he stopped me. "Lee, so sorry, but it can't come out or it will get dirty by hitting the underside of the table all the time and I want it to be clean for you."

My mouth dropped.

"Sorry." he chuckled.

"Oh no. I understand. It's okay. Really." I looked around at the others. Dree and Bree had their hands under the table, but they weren't on their men. From what I could tell, they were stroking themselves while they talked and sipped and ate.

Akello rubbed my leg. "See the other girls? They all have the same problem with their men and so the men have asked the ladies to keep their fires burning and to edge repeatedly to be able to have greater pleasure later. The men could do it for them, but their hands are hard and too big to not eventually make the ladies sore. Might I suggest you do the same?"

He took my hand and slid it over my dress until he found my hardness beneath the fluff. He wrapped my fingers around it. "Please. It would please me greatly to see you please yourself while we chatted. It would be a compliment to me and be very sexy."

I stroked it, gazing lovingly into his eyes.

"That a girl. You're such a sweet girl to do that for me. Bring yourself to the edge if you can." He grazed my neck with his breath and sniffed my hair while his hand squeezed my thigh. I sped up my jerking. "That's it. Good girl," he whispered in my ear. "Feel it. Imagine me inside of your sweet tightness. Imagine me depositing my passion into your lovely body." He pulled his head back from my neck, looked around at the others doing similar things as Dree and Bree jerked off. He watched me jerk it. A look of love in his eyes. "Good girl."

He leaned back and crossed his legs beneath the table and put both hands on the table, then took his drink and watched me. I played with myself and gasped as I came to the edge, looking into his eyes, then stopped and let it go.

He patted my thigh. "There. Good. Wait a bit, then begin again." He gave me a peck on the cheek. "Such a sweet little girl you are. I'm so honored to be with you and have you doing this for me."

I ate some oysters and crab and learned more about Akello's life and education, likes and dislikes. He was an incredibly interesting man with diverse talents and interests. I was falling in love with him.

When we were done with appetizers, we had a light refreshing drink they selected for us and Akello once more had me please myself, like Bree and Dree were again doing while we talked and he leaned back and enjoyed the show I was giving him. I did it proudly, since he loved me doing it so much, and it was almost impossible not to do it while being near him, anyway. His eyes on me as I jerked off to him sent ripples of pleasure into me and filled me with the passion he had for me. It was more stimulating than actually jerking my little girl was.

Dinner went on like that and I believe I came to the edge at least thirty times through all of it... and desert... and absinthe... and espressos. Before we finished dinner, Akello, Bale, and Dembe even joined us girls in moderately pleasing themselves through their pants and the six of us were like an adolescent jerk fest, but without coming. By the time we had finished and the men paid the bill, we were all very much on the edge and very much wanting to release all of our pent up passion for each other.

After us girls excused ourselves to the bathroom and softened enough to pee, we touched up our makeup and perfume and headed back to the men. My heart raced and my little girl throbbed and bounced as I anticipated what glorious night was to come with Akello inside of me.

10

In the limo, we released the men from their pants for a while and we all sucked them delightedly. I needed both hands, and I still didn't cover the length of Akello's shaft with my mouth stretched wide and taking in as much as I could and still be able to run my tongue around it and bob my head on it. It had to be ten inches long and almost as thick as a can of soda.

The skin was velvety smooth, and it was hard as a rock and the tip oozed sweet saltiness constantly. He made me stop twice to save it and I'd stare at it, bobbing freely in the air, huge shaved globes beneath it. It was truly glorious.

They drove us to their hotel, and they said their driver could deliver us home in the late morning if we wanted to stay with them. We couldn't resist.

The men exited the car and carried their coats over their arm before them to hide their tent poles while we made our way to the elevators. The men opened their adjoining rooms and us girls all gave one last grin to each other as the men carried us over the threshold and into their rooms.

Akello poured us drinks, and we sat on the couch. His eyes roamed my face, hair, body. My eyes locked on his hard cock in his pants, where my hand rubbed it. "It's incredible. Can we go into the bedroom now?"

"Of course." He stood and took me by the hand. He pulled back the covers, revealing satin sheets, then sat on a chair in the corner and undid his shoes. I slid onto the bed and up against the headboard, watching him strip. He folded his clothes neatly as he revealed his lithe yet muscular frame, each hairless and silky curve and bulge, shining like polished ebony in the light from the lamp on the nightstand.

I slid off the bed and hurried into the bathroom to freshen up and pee, then sprayed perfume over me and checked myself in the mirror. Digging in my purse, I found the tube of lube and slid it between my butt cheeks, and squirted some into my hole. My heart pounded as I thought of what was about to happen. How I'd be penetrated, filled, and used as a receptacle for a black man's passion. I throbbed under my dress; the tip rubbing the fabric with each leap.

I walked in minced steps over to the bed where Akello laid back against the headboard, his teeth flashing his anticipation, his eyes taking me in, his tent pole leaping and dropping before him. It drew me to it like a magnet.

I glided my hand over his powerful thigh and upward to cup his hairless globes and roll them in my hand while my other hand did its best to wrap my fingers around the velvet shaft as far as my fingers could go. I squeezed it and stroked it, admiring it while a pearl rose through the tip and slid down the side. Licking it off, I opened my jaw as far as it would go, then took as much of it into my face as I could while gazing up subserviently into his loving eyes.

The sensation in my mouth as I bobbed and sucked and ran my tongue around the shaft was as if my mouth was a sex organ and that electric sensation permeated my mouth and filled my soul. I stroked it with my other hand while rolling his globes and it was as if I was pumping the sensations into my face. We were electrically connected, and this was only my mouth.

He moaned. "Lee, are you ready for me?"

I nodded and mumbled around his shaft, not wanting to let go of it. He tugged me off of it, freeing it to gleam, all wet, in the light. Akello slid around behind me and wrapped his legs on either side of me, then lifted me off the bed. He slid it between my legs and butt cheeks, then lifted me by the hips, picking me up off the ground and bending me in two so my hands were on the floor.

Guiding the thick tip against my hole, he pressed it against it and held my hips to press me onto it slowly. He pressed and stretched me, then backed off and pressed me onto it again. He did this, going slightly deeper each time, making me wonder if I would truly split in two. There was some pain, but it was a thrilling pain when the tip finally made me gasp as it breached the gate and spread me wide.

"Are you okay, my love?"

I nodded, dangling by my hip and looking up from at him over my shoulder like a rag doll in his arms. "Please, go deeper."

He held my hips fast and pressed. The pain left and a sense of connectedness gave me ripples of sensation through my body, making a leg twitch. He stood straight up and dangled me like a sack of grain as he began thrusting into me, going deeper and deeper. My hard little girl flailed in the air beneath me, sweeping back and forth against the silky lining of the dress. I heard myself whimper in a little girl's voice.

"Are you well?"

I nodded. "Oh god I'm excellent."

I squeaked after the next thrust and he began in earnest to shove that thing into me over and over while I dangled from my hips, my legs dangling, my head dangling and swinging. I was a little-girl-doll, and he was using me. He moaned and grunted, "You are such a tight and sweet little doll. Such a wonderful girl. I'm trying to hold it back. Play with yourself a bit. Don't finish though."

I grabbed my little girl and jerked her while he drew his magnificent manhood almost all the way out, then plunged it all the way up to my throat. I was oozing and had to let go of my little girl and let her flail in her nest and the cool air.

He lifted me by lifting my legs up by the ankles, bending me with my feet by my face, then rotated me on his shaft and brought us to the bed. He lay me back, then pressed my thighs back, my stilettos dangling by my ears. I could see his face now and could see the proud beast as it split my cheeks in two and repeatedly dashed into the cave, then retreated again.

I looked into his eyes, his bare chest shining in the light while he looked lovingly into my eyes and thrusted over and over, making me unthinkingly whimper and squeak like some sort of blow up sex doll. "You sound so wonderfully tiny and helpless and in such bliss. That's it, my love. Experience my passion for you. Steal it from me. Tell me what you want."

I heard my little sounds ushering from me in time with him. In gasps and choppy breath I spoke in a tiny voice, "I... want you to... come... inside of me. I want you to... *breed* me. Make me your wife. Fill me... with your seed. I want to you.... pulsing in me." Whimpers and squeaks continued.

He grunted and moaned and thrusted like a bull. My legs tense, my toes pointed in their heels, flailing in the air above me. His huge hand held me fast to the bed. His breathing was heavy, mine was choppy, taken in gasps between squeals and whimpers.

"Here we go, little girl. My sweet sissy girl."

It sounded so perfect in his accent. I had an epiphany. I was a *sissy girl* now, and I *loved* it. "Akello. Say it again! Call me that."

"My little *sissy girl*. Lee is my little sissy girl."

His eyes went wide. He drew it almost all the way out, then shoved it hard and deep and his legs tensed as he let out a low guttural groan and his flag pole began pulsing inside of me. "Breeding my sissy girl."

My little girl, in its nest of ruffles and lace, leapt and spewed a rope of pearls across my belly and onto my face and hair. He drew back and shoved again and it was as if he pumped his juice through me to shoot out of my little girl again, hitting my hair and mouth. I licked my come from my lips and as he pulsed inside of me again; I looked down to see another rope fly toward me and I opened my mouth to catch it.

He groaned and his pulsing subsided. He moved it slowly and deliciously inside of me as he peppered my face with kisses and let my legs fall to the side. I wrapped them around his hard ass and pulled him into me, sniffing his sweet, cologned chest.

He collapsed on me and I lay there, pinned to the bed, as we both caught our breath. I felt his seed dripping down my butt cheek and mine slipping down my face. He lifted himself off of me and went into the bathroom. The shower started. I went in and washed my face and brushed my teeth. I had no clothes to change into and didn't want to sleep naked, so I slid under the satin sheet and soon, showered and fresh, he spooned me.

11

I woke in the morning with the realization of what had happened and where I was. I turned to look over and Akello was sleeping peacefully. I ran my hand under the sheet and onto his thigh, then glided it up to grasp his limp, heavy snake. I lifted the sheet, having a strong desire to have it grow in my mouth.

I took the thick soft shaft and sucked it into my mouth like a large noodle, then ran my tongue around it while looking at his face. His eyes opened, and a smile filled his face while his snake grew and firmed up in my mouth. Soon, it was too large to take it all in and I began using my hands on it and opened my jaw wide, guarding my teeth with my lips and I bobbed, sucked, rolled his globes, stroked, and ran my tongue around it.

"Come with me, Lee. Jerk your sissyness for me and show me how excited I make you and let me see you come with me, my little sissy girl."

His words raised the level of my arousal to the peak as I jerked myself like an adolescent while sucking this perfect example of a real man, only wishing to make him feel wonderful. I needed to make him feel so good he comes for me. I became fervent and diligent in my ministrations while looking up into his eyes, watching his response to me, my mouth stretched almost painfully wide open upon his glorious pole.

He looked down at me and cradled my head. "Such a sweet sissy girl you are Lee. It looks so perfect going into your sweet face while you struggle to open your mouth wide enough. May I take a picture for you so you can see and I can keep it as a remembrance?"

I mumbled around it, "Please, yes," and nodded.

He reached over, took his phone, and snapped a few pics, then turned it to video. "That's it, my sissy girl. Take your reward from me while toying with your sissy cock and make your little girl squirt." He leaned back to capture me in the video as I jerked my little girl furiously and ministered to his epitome of maleness, desperately, my eyes wide with drive and passion. I looked into the lens, my eyes wide open, my mouth stretched around it, bobbing and sucking and rolling his globes in my palm, while my other hand stroked the unsucked portion.

It pulsed under my grip and into my mouth, then I struggled to gulp it down, my eyes closing, then blinking furiously as another and another massive gush shot into me. My little girl shot ropes onto my dress while I stroked it. We both tensed and I whimpered around his glorious shaft in my mouth as some of his pearly passion leaked out and down my chin.

When we both stopped shuddering, he stopped taking video and put his phone down. He kissed me on the head and lifted me from his maleness to hug me and embrace me. He looked at the clock on the nightstand. "It's time to go. I need to get ready to leave. Give me your phone number and I'll text you the video and we can stay in touch if you like."

I hurriedly leapt to my purse, took my phone out and said, "Your number?" He shot it off, and I entered it. He tapped his phone a few times and put it down. "They're on the way. Wait until you see how gorgeous you look."

He came over to me and gave me a bear hug, lifting me off the ground. His flaccid meat flopped against my dress. I took it in my hand and looked into his eyes. "Thank you. All of it was heavenly. I wish I could go to Uganda with you."

He nodded with a sad look. Ran his hand over my hair and touched the side of my cheek with the back of his hand. "Yes, that would be lovely. Unfortunately, it isn't safe for you there yet. It might take years before it is. We'll have to be happy with a visit now and then."

I nodded. Tears welled up, and I pulled away and straightened my dress in the mirror and slung my purse. I wiped a drip from my chin and licked my finger. Wearing pants and a shirt now, he held the door open. I stood on my tiptoes and gave him a peck on the lips. I left and walked down the hall.

12

Bree, Dree, and I sat silently in the back of the Limo, all of us looking sad. Bree drew in a shaky breath and looked out the window and wiped her eyes. Dree's head rested on her hand as she gazed emptily out the window.

The driver opened our door at Bree and Dree's house and we all exited the Limo.

"Come in for a coffee and breakfast?" Bree asked.

I shook my head. "Nah. Thanks. Gonna have some cake and coffee at home, then get cleaned up. Later? Lunch?"

"Sure."

I walked in my minced steps down the sidewalk to my house. I must have looked like a wayward hooker in the outfit and heels I wore. Hooker... I laughed. Sissy.... Hooker... I guess it fit a bit. Slutty little girl or sissy fuck doll might fit better, though. In any case. I was happy I was whatever I was. It was a hell of a lot more interesting than what I used to be. Now, I was living my fantasy, and I almost pinched myself so I'd know it was real. It all had happened. I was *Full-Filled*. What was next for me?

13

The doorbell chimed through its paces. Bree's smiling face appeared at the door. "C'mon in sweetie."

I stepped in, my boots clunking on the floor. She grabbed my arm and a look of shock appeared on her face. A grin spread. "What's this?" She motioned with her hand up and down my body.

"It's a break. I needed to wear jeans and not do makeup and keep things simple. I kept my nails!" I waved my hands in front of her, showing them. "Panties, girls' jeans, perfume. Don't worry, I'm still all girl, just laid back a little." I patted my chest. "No boobs, just a bra. Those forms are a nuisance. I'm gonna need to get implants like yours."

Her eyes lit up. "You'll get a discount. She's great at it too. Quick healing."

I nodded. "K, give me the info later and I'll set it up soon, so I'm done by the start of school. After last night, I knew what I was, and it sure wasn't a guy. I never was a guy. I'm a cute little sissy girl like Akeloo calls me." A tear welled in my eye.

Bree's hand rested on my shoulder and soothed me. "It's okay. It'll pass. We'll find others. We have each other, too."

Dree came in wearing boy's jeans and clothes and gave me a hug. "I can be the guy for both of you."

I had to laugh. "Okay cutie. Whatever you say." I pecked him on the lips and gave him a hug. "Right Bree? So Dree is gonna be our boyfriend for now. Think he'll do for us?"

Bree looked him up and down. She grabbed his crotch and made a face. "Hmm, I suppose. If we get bored, we'll just dress him up like a little barbie doll and the three of us will go out and find something more intriguing. So... go to the park and take a nap on a blanket in the shade by the lake?"

We all held hands and walked out of the house. I had been *Full-Filled* and now I was fulfilled.

If you enjoyed this book, it would be great if you could leave a review and tell a friend about it or blog it out. Thanks!

Barb and Thom

For more of our books, both fiction and non-fiction, in Kindle, paperback and Audible versions, go to:

Amazon:

http://www.amazon.com/Barbara-Deloto/e/B00J21HWA4/

Made in the USA
Columbia, SC
04 May 2025

57530132R10033